STAR WARS

ESCAPE FROM DARTH VADER

WRITTEN BY MICHAEL SIGLAIN

ART BY STEPHANE ROUX

EGMONT
We bring stories to life

First published in Great Britain 2015
by Egmont UK Limited, The Yellow Building,
1 Nicholas Road, London W11 4AN.

ISBN 978 1 4052 7777 8
60529/2
Printed in Singapore

To find more great *Star Wars* books, visit www.egmont.co.uk/starwars

Stay safe online. Any website addresses listed in this book are correct at the
time of going to print. However, Egmont is not responsible for content hosted
by third parties. Please be aware that online content can be subject to change
and websites can contain content that is unsuitable for children.
We advise that all children are supervised
when using the internet.

Long ago
and far, far away . . .

a small ship was under attack.

It was being chased by a big ship.

Inside the small ship were two droids.

One droid was short,
and the other was tall.

The tall droid
was named C-3PO.

He was worried.

He thought they

were doomed.

The short droid
was named R2-D2.

He was not worried.

He wanted to find the princess.

The princess
was named Leia.

Princess Leia had
secret battle plans.

The troopers

from the big ship

wanted to steal the
secret battle plans.

The troopers
ran through the
small ship.

Then Darth Vader appeared.

Darth Vader was a Sith Lord.
He was mean and scary.

Darth Vader ordered
the troopers to
search the ship.

Princess Leia had to
keep the secret plans
hidden from Darth Vader.

She gave them to R2-D2
to keep them safe.

Then Princess Leia
hid from Darth Vader.

But the troopers
were still looking
for the princess.

Princess Leia attacked the troopers.

But the troopers
captured her.
They brought her to
Darth Vader.

The princess did not
tell Darth Vader that
R2-D2 had the plans.

No one knew where R2-D2 was.

Then C-3PO found him.

R2-D2 got inside an escape pod.

He had to get the plans off the ship.

C-3PO followed R2-D2 into the pod.

The pod flew away from the big ship.

The droids escaped
from Darth Vader!

They landed on a
very sandy planet.

Now a new journey was about to begin for R2-D2 and C-3PO!